EGMONT

We bring stories to life

Thomas the Tank Engine & Friends™

CREATED BY BRITT ALLCROFT

Based on the Railway Series by the Reverend W Awdry
© 2011 Gullane (Thomas) LLC. A HIT Entertainment company.
Thomas the Tank Engine & Friends and Thomas & Friends are trademarks of Gullane (Thomas) Limited.
Thomas the Tank Engine & Friends and Design is Reg. U.S. Pat. & Tm. Off.

HiT entertainment

First published in Great Britain 2011 by Egmont UK Limited,
239 Kensington High Street, London W8 6SA

ISBN: 978 0 6035 6636 3
1 3 5 7 9 10 8 6 4 2
Printed in Italy

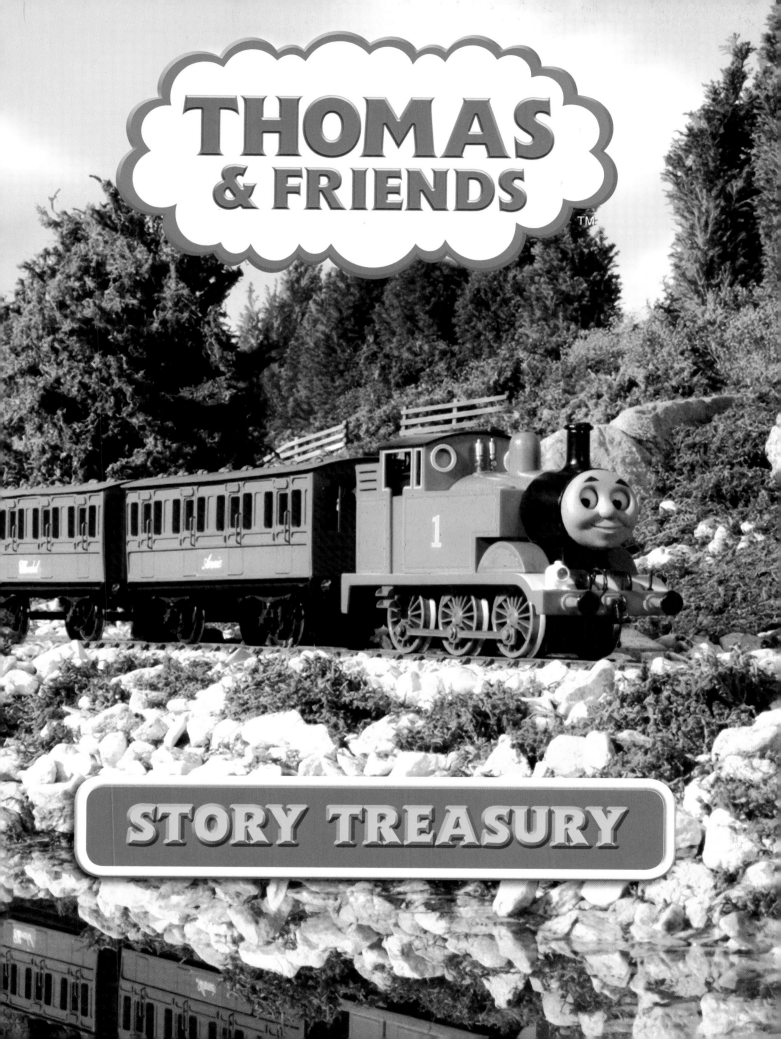

This Story Treasury belongs to

....

Contents

Thomas' New Trucks

It was another busy day on the Island of Sodor. Thomas was in the Yard, shunting his trucks. It was hard work and he was **huffing** and **puffing**, **biffing** and **bashing** the trucks. They were old and rusty and Thomas was tired out.

When James puffed into the Yard, he was looking very pleased with himself. "Look!" he huffed proudly. "The Fat Controller has given me shiny new trucks. They're **MUCH** nicer than your old ones, Thomas!"

Thomas looked at the trucks. James was right, the new ones were much nicer than his. "It's not fair!" said Thomas sadly. "I want shiny new trucks, too!"

The next morning, when Thomas puffed out of Tidmouth Sheds, The Fat Controller had a surprise for him. "Your trucks are too old for the heavy loads you pull, Thomas," he said. "You're going to have some new ones, just like James."

Thomas was very pleased when he collected his trucks. He puffed off proudly with his new trucks behind him.

As he steamed into Brendam Docks, James was showing off his new trucks to Bill and Ben.

"**Peep!**" said Thomas, blowing his whistle. "I've got new trucks, too!"

"Yours are even shinier than James'!" puffed Ben.

That made James cross. "Your trucks are shiny now, Thomas," he huffed. "But you won't be able to keep them as clean and shiny as mine!"

"Oh yes I will!" said Thomas. "You wait and see. I'll have the cleanest, shiniest trucks on the whole Island!"

Next day, Thomas took his new trucks to the Quarry. "**Must-keep-my-trucks-clean! Must-keep-my-trucks-clean!**" he puffed.

James was there collecting slate. "Look, I haven't got a speck of dust on me **OR** my trucks!" he boasted.

"I can do that, too!" said Thomas. He backed under a hopper but his naughty new trucks rolled back a bit too far and – **whooosh!** – slate poured down all over the tracks, and all over Thomas!

The new trucks laughed, and so did James. "Your trucks don't look so shiny now!" he huffed.

Next, Thomas took his new trucks to the Coaling Plant. This time he backed under the coal hopper VERY slowly. But the naughty trucks rolled too far again and the coal landed all over the tracks. Thomas was covered in coal dust and his new trucks were dirtier than ever!

The next morning, Thomas puffed into Wellsworth Yard. He saw his new trucks **AND** his old ones and had an idea. "I'll use my old trucks for the messy coal, and keep my new ones clean," he decided.

He took his old trucks to the Docks, but on the way, there was trouble! A coupling broke – **SNAP!** – and the trucks rattled along behind him all by themselves!

"**Cinders and ashes!**" cried Thomas. He put on his brakes but he stopped so quickly that the trucks bumped into him and all the coal spilled out on to the tracks. Thomas was stuck. He couldn't move!

When The Fat Controller arrived with Harvey, he was not pleased! "These trucks are too old for pulling coal," he said. "You've caused a delay, Thomas!"

Harvey moved the spilled coal and Thomas raced off to collect his trucks.

When he got back, the crew filled them with coal.

Soon the new trucks were very dirty. But as Thomas raced to the Docks they were no trouble at all.

They rolled easily up the hills ... They rattled quickly down the hills ... And they sang all the way to the Docks! They were happy!

Thomas understood. "My new trucks **LIKE** being messy," he said. "They have more fun when they're dirty! My trucks would rather be **USEFUL** than **clean**!"

When James got to the Docks and his trucks saw how happy Thomas' were, they decided they wanted some fun too.

James backed up to Cranky to load melons for the market but his trucks stopped **VERY** quickly.

"Hold back! Hold back!" they laughed as the melons landed on James. *Squelch! Squish! Squash!* What a sticky mess!

"**Bother!**" huffed James but his trucks just laughed, and so did Thomas.

"**Peep!**" said Thomas. "Your trucks would rather be **USEFUL** than clean, just like mine!"

Thomas and the Treasure

Brendam Docks is a very busy place. Engines move goods trucks there, cranes unload cargo, and ships bring visitors.

One day, Thomas went there to collect a very important visitor – the Admiral! He was going to open the new Maritime Museum, and Thomas was taking him there.

Salty said, "I've seen the Admiral before. He comes to Sodor to look for the pirate treasure that's hidden here!"

"Pirates?" said James.
"Treasure?" said Emily.
"Rubbish!" said Henry.

"Oh, yes," said Salty. "There's pirate treasure here, but no one has ever found it!"

Salty told them more. "There are three clues that lead to the treasure," he said. "First, find the **eagle of the mountains**. Its beak points to the **clouds that are not in the sky**. They show the way to the **skull and crossbones**! And there you'll find the treasure, me hearties!"

Emily and James thought Salty was being silly!

But Thomas didn't. "**Eagle ... clouds ... skull and crossbones ...**" he tooted. "I'm sure I can find those clues!"

Thomas puffed off. "What if I get to the Museum with the Admiral **and** a chest of pirate treasure?" he said. "That will show the others!"

Thomas chuffed along a track that went to the mountains. He was going to look for the first clue!

"Where will I find an eagle?" said Thomas. "How can clouds not be in the sky? And where will I find a skull and crossbones?"

Later, Emily puffed up to Thomas. "There's no buried treasure!" she laughed.

But Thomas took no notice of her.

Suddenly, Thomas saw a mountain that was shaped like an eagle!

"I've found the first clue!" he peeped happily. "Salty said the eagle's beak points to the next one!"

There was a track in front of the stone beak so Thomas chuffed along it.

James saw him. "Where are you going, Thomas?" he wheeshed.

"To find the clouds that are not in the sky!" whistled Thomas.

James snorted. "Oh, how silly!"

Thomas didn't care, because he soon found the clouds! They weren't in the sky. They were reflections in the lake!

"**Peep!**" said Thomas. "The second clue! I need to solve one more to find the treasure!"

Thomas searched and searched. He forgot all about the Admiral! He was still looking when Harold arrived with The Fat Controller.

"The Admiral is late for the opening of the Maritime Museum!" The Fat Controller told Thomas. "You have been unreliable. Harold will take him now."

Thomas felt bad. He knew he had spent too much time looking for clues.

"Fancy believing in a silly old story!" laughed Harold.

"Everyone thinks I'm silly," huffed Thomas. "But I still believe in the treasure!"

He puffed along the track that led away from the lake. He had never been this way before. He didn't know that it led into … a tunnel!

Thomas chuffed through it and came out at the Maritime Museum!

"I am proud to open the Maritime Museum!" said the Admiral.

Everyone cheered.

"Peep!" said Thomas. "The pirate treasure is here!"

"Don't be silly, Thomas!" huffed Emily.

"It's just a silly old story!" snorted James.

But Thomas knew he was right. "Look at the rocks! It's the skull and crossbones!" he puffed.

"Yes!" said the Admiral. "Someone get me a shovel!"

The Admiral dug down into the sand and found a big wooden chest. Inside there were jewels and pearls and lots of gold coins.

"The treasure will be the most important thing in the whole Maritime Museum!" said the Admiral.

"Well done, Thomas," said The Fat Controller.

Thomas felt very proud. He had been right to believe Salty's story! He had found the pirate treasure!

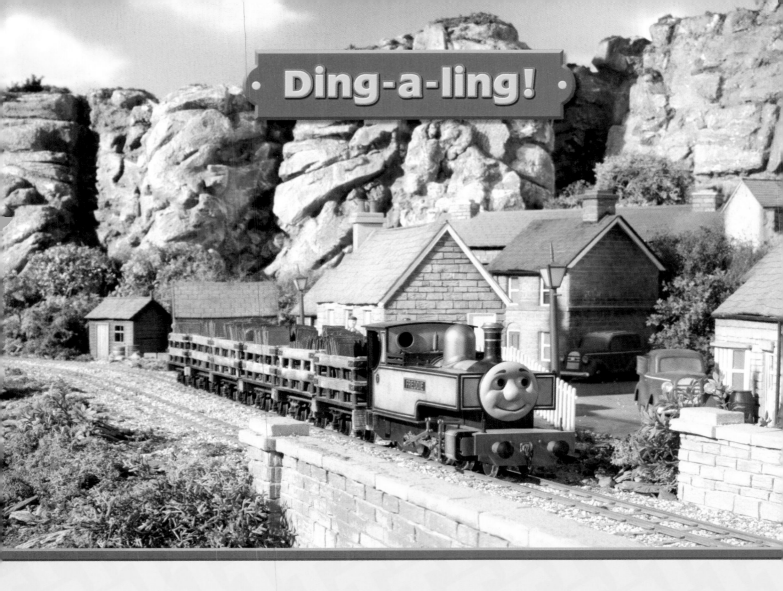

· Ding-a-ling! ·

One bright spring morning, Freddie, the old mountain engine, arrived at the Wharf to collect a new bicycle for Mr Percival, The Thin Controller.

When James steamed in with the bicycle, Freddie whistled. **"Peep! Peep! You're late, James!"**

"I came as fast as I could!" wheeshed James, crossly.

Soon, the bicycle was loaded on to Freddie's flatbed.

"The bicycle doesn't have a bell!" James huffed. "A bicycle bell is like an engine whistle. It lets everyone know you're there! You must find one right away!"

Freddie didn't know where to find a bell, but he didn't want James to know that.

"I'll find a bicycle bell!" Freddie whistled, and he puffed away.

Freddie chuffed along. "Ding-a-ling, ding-a-ling!" he sang. **"I'll find a bell with the very best ring!"**

Freddie stopped when he saw a farmer with his cows.

"Hooray!" he smiled. "A cow bell will be just as good as a bicycle bell!"

The farmer hung the cow bell on the handlebars as Mighty Mac puffed up. **DING, DONG,** the cow bell rang.

"Listen to that!" called Freddie proudly. "It's nice and loud."

But the cows didn't even look up.

"The cows are taking no notice of the bell!" scoffed Mighty Mac. "It's no use as a bicycle bell!"

Freddie chuffed off to the Top Station where he met Cuffie the Clown. He had lots of bells around his neck.

"Hooray!" said Freddie. "Cuffie's bells will be just as good for a bicycle bell!"

Cuffie hung the bells next to the cow bell as Peter Sam puffed up.

JINGLE, JANGLE, Cuffie's bells tinkled.

"Listen to that!" whistled Freddie, proudly.

But the children were watching Cuffie.

"The children are taking no notice of the bells!" puffed Peter Sam. "They're no use as a bicycle bell!"

Poor Freddie! "I'll have to go back to the Wharf and tell them all that I can't find a bell," said Freddie, sadly.

But when he got there, he saw a shiny new school bell!

"Hooray!" he whistled. "A big school bell is even better than a little bicycle bell!"

A workman put the bell on the bicycle. But it was so heavy that the bicycle toppled off the flatbed, and crashed to the ground, **DING, DONG, JINGLE, JANGLE!**

The Yard Manager was cross. "The Thin Controller is waiting for his new bicycle!" he said. "I'll have all the bells taken off, then you must deliver it to him, Freddie."

Soon after, Freddie was puffing out of the Wharf when Thomas chuffed in with a shiny foghorn. "It's an old bell that's been polished," Thomas told him. "It's as good as new."

"Now I know what to do!" cried Freddie. He had an idea.

Later on, Freddie delivered The Thin Controller's new bicycle. He had asked the Yard Manager to clean and polish the bell from Mr Percival's old bicycle and put it on his new one! **"What a good idea, Freddie!"** said The Thin Controller. He was very happy with his new bell, and rang it, **ding-a-ling!**

Tuneful Toots

The little engines who work on the Narrow Gauge mountain railway are always busy! They go **up** the hills and **down** the hills, all day long!

Rusty likes puffing along by the lake best. He likes to toot his horn there because the sound echoes around the hills.

Rusty's horn is special because it has two notes, a high one and a low one: *"Toot! Toot!"*

Rusty liked his toot, but the other engines didn't. They thought it was the most awful noise they had ever heard!

One morning Mr Percival, The Thin Controller of the Narrow Gauge railway, had news for the engines. "Sir Topham and Lady Hatt are visiting our railway tonight," he told them. "And a brass band is coming to play for them!"

The engines were very excited. Rusty loved brass-band music and couldn't wait to hear it.

There was a lot to do before the visit, though!

Skarloey and Rheneas brought tables and chairs and Duncan and Peter Sam helped too.

Rusty thought he had the best job of all! He was going to take the members of the brass band on a trip before the concert started. When he pulled into the Transfer Yards to collect them, he tooted his horn happily: ***"Toot! Toot!"***

Thomas heard the toot when he arrived with the bandstand. "What was that lovely sound?" he asked.

"It was Rusty," Peter Sam told him. "He thinks his horn is special, but we don't like it!"

"Wheesh!" said Thomas. "Well I do!"

When the brass band players were on board, Rusty pulled out of the station.

"Don't be back late!" called The Thin Controller, but Rusty didn't hear him. He was too busy tooting his horn: ***"Toot! Toot! Toot! Toot! Toot! Toot!"***

Rusty took the brass band to the viaduct and the bridge. He was so happy that he forgot all about the concert and set off for the lake!

Clickety-clack! went Rusty as he huffed past the old castle: *"Toot! Toot!"*

But suddenly – **clang!** – Rusty stopped. He had run out of fuel!

"How will we get back?" said the leader of the band. "How will Mr Percival know where we are?"

Rusty tooted. "If you all play loudly and I toot my horn extra hard, the sound will echo all the way back to the Yards," he said. "Then The Thin Controller will know where we are."

The leader of the band waved his baton and the band began to play. Then Rusty tooted his horn as loudly as he could:

"Toot! Toot!"

"Toot! Toot!"

"Toot! Toot!"

Thomas and The Fat Controller and Lady Hatt were waiting in the Transfer Yards when they heard the sounds.

"That's Rusty and the brass band!" puffed Thomas. "They must be in trouble. If we follow the sounds, we'll find them."

The brass band kept playing and Rusty kept tooting until he saw engine lamps coming towards them along the track.

Soon all the engines were at the lake, and so was The Fat Controller. "We will have the brass band concert here!" he said.

"We heard your horn, Rusty!" said Peter Sam.

"That's how we found you!" said Duncan.

"Because you have a really special tooty horn!" said Skarloey. Rusty was very pleased and when all the engines blew their whistles – **"PEEP!"** – Rusty tooted louder than ever before:

"Toot! Toot!"

Thomas and the jet plane

Thomas loves having buffers that **biff** and **bash** and a boiler that **bubbles**. He loves having **clickety-clackety** wheels and a whistle that goes **peep**.

But most of all Thomas loves being a Really Useful Engine on The Fat Controller's railway.

On the day of the Sodor Summer Picnic, The Fat Controller had a special job for him.

"I want you to collect the children from the Airport and bring them to the picnic," he said.

"Yes, Sir!" said Thomas.

He set off right away.

The Airport was new and all the engines wanted to go there. Thomas was pleased that he had been chosen.

When he got there, he heard a loud noise. **Whoosh!** A big jet plane was coming in to land!

"**Peep!**" said Thomas, and he chuffed over to say hello. "I'm Thomas," he said. "I'm a tank engine."

"Hello," said the plane. "I'm Jeremy. I'm a jet plane."

"Flying must be wonderful," said Thomas.

"Oh, it is!" said Jeremy. "I can go anywhere I like! Anywhere!"

"I like travelling on tracks," Thomas huffed. "I puff past farms and villages."

"But when I'm up in the air I can see the whole Island all at once!" Jeremy boasted.

Thomas took the children to the picnic. He thought Jeremy was a bit of a show-off. "I never want to talk to that jumped-up jet plane again!" he huffed.

Thomas went round a bend in the track and had to stop at a signal.

Whoosh! Jeremy flew right over his funnel!

"It's not fair!" huffed Thomas. "Jeremy doesn't have to stop at signals."

Thomas puffed away but soon had to stop as there was a cow on the tracks in front of him! He put on his brakes sharply.

"It's not fair," said Thomas. "Jet planes don't have to stop for cows."

Everyone had a good time at the picnic. Everyone but Thomas …

"What's wrong?" asked his friend, Percy, who puffed up beside Thomas.

"Planes can go wherever they like. I can't. I wish I was a jet plane," said Thomas.

"But engines can pull carriages, and take children to picnics," peeped Percy. "Engines are Really Useful!"

But Thomas wasn't so sure …

Jeremy flew to the Mainland. But when big black clouds filled the sky he had to go back to the Airport. It wasn't safe to fly.

Thomas was chuffing past the Airport when Jeremy landed. Thomas didn't want to talk to him.

But Jeremy said, "Thomas! There's a big rain storm coming. The children's picnic will be ruined!"

"Cinders and ashes!" cried Thomas. "I'll tell The Fat Controller!"

Thomas got to the picnic just in time. "Quick!" he peeped. "There's a big rain storm coming. Pack up the picnic!"

The children packed up the food and sat in Thomas' coaches, Annie and Clarabel.

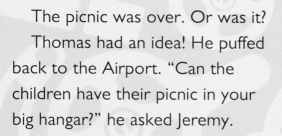

The picnic was over. Or was it? Thomas had an idea! He puffed back to the Airport. "Can the children have their picnic in your big hangar?" he asked Jeremy.

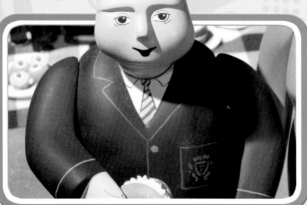

"Of course they can!" said Jeremy. "Come in!"

The children had a lovely time. And so did The Fat Controller.

"Well done, Thomas and Jeremy!" he said. "You have saved the picnic. You are both **Really Useful!"**

Thomas felt very proud. So did Jeremy!

Thomas Sets Sail

It was spring on the Island of Sodor, and a cold wind blew.

But Thomas hardly noticed the wind. He had an important job to do at Brendam Docks.

The Mayor of Sodor had a new sailing boat, and Thomas was taking it to be launched. The Mayor, The Fat Controller and Lady Hatt – and Thomas! – were going to watch the boat go into the sea for the very first time!

When Thomas got to the Docks, Gordon and James were admiring the boat.

"It's bright red, just like me!" huffed James, crossly. "I should be taking it!"

"It's big and heavy," wheeshed Gordon. "A strong engine like me should be taking it!"

Cranky the Crane put the boat on Thomas' flatbed.

"You must wait for the engineer to lower the mast," Cranky told Thomas.

But Thomas took no notice. "The mast will be no trouble for me!" he said, racing away.

The wind was strong, and the boat was heavy. But not too heavy for Thomas! **"I can do it, I can do it!"** he puffed.

Thomas felt very proud as he steamed past Emily.

"Be careful, Thomas!" she tooted. "It's very windy!"

But Thomas took no notice of her!

When Thomas puffed towards a low bridge, Rosie tooted to warn him.

"Be careful, Thomas!" she said. "The mast is too tall to go under the bridge!"

"Then I'll take another track!" huffed Thomas.

But when he did, there was trouble! **CRUNCH, CREAK!** "Oh, no!" cried Thomas. "The mast is caught in the trees."

Thomas huffed, then he chuffed, and with a mighty pull, he broke free.

But the ropes had come undone. Now Thomas had big white sails, just like a boat!

The wind blew him along, faster and faster.

The Mayor and The Fat Controller were waiting at the Harbour, as Thomas raced towards them.

"Slow down, Thomas!" boomed The Fat Controller.

But Thomas **couldn't** slow down! He whooshed past the platform, and raced away down the track.

When the wind stopped blowing, Thomas managed to stop as well.

"If it blows again, I won't be able to stop at the Harbour," he said. "The boat will not be launched, and The Fat Controller will be cross!"

Thomas knew what he had to do. The crew uncoupled him from the flatbed, and he steamed off back to the Docks.

Then he brought the Engineer back to the boat to roll up the sails and lower the mast.

When Thomas chuffed back to the Harbour, the Mayor and The Fat Controller were still waiting for him.

Everyone smiled as the boat was launched on the water. **Splash!**

"Phew!" said Thomas. He was pleased he had not caused an accident. Next time he would listen when others told him to be careful.

Saving Edward

It was summer on Sodor and the engines were busy taking passengers and goods all over the Island. Thomas, Gordon and the other engines were happy to be so Useful.

But Edward wasn't happy. He was worried because he didn't feel well. He wheezed as he puffed along and steam hissed out of his cylinders.

One morning, The Fat Controller went to Tidmouth Sheds. He had jobs for Edward and Thomas. "Edward, I want you to take a special delivery of fruit and vegetables from the Docks to Knapford," he said. "Thomas, I want you to go to the Docks and shunt Edward's trucks."

Thomas and Edward puffed to the water tower to take on water. But Edward just couldn't stop wheezing.

"You don't sound well," said Thomas.

"I can't get up steam properly," hissed Edward. "But please don't tell anyone, Thomas. I don't want The Fat Controller to know."

Edward puffed to the Docks but it took him a long time to get there because he could only go slowly. As he wheezed along he felt more and more worried. What if he was too weak to pull his train? He would be no use at all.

"Must-keep-going! Must-keep-going!" he wheezed.

At the Docks, Thomas shunted Edward's trucks for him and soon he was ready to go.

Edward puffed as hard as he could but the train moved very slowly – then it stopped. "I'm sorry," he wheezed. "I'm not a Really Useful engine any more. I'll just have to go for scrap."

Thomas wanted to help his old friend. "I'll do my other jobs first," he told him. "Then I'll come back and pull the train for you."

Poor Edward! He could only stand and wait for Thomas to come back ...

Thomas did his other jobs as fast as he could.

"Hurry-up! Hurry-up!" he told the Troublesome Trucks.

"What-for? What-for?" snapped the trucks.

"For Edward!" said Thomas, **biffing** them into a siding.

When Thomas got back to the Docks, Edward was very pleased to see him.

"I'll be back for you soon," said Thomas, then puffed off with Edward's train.

But Edward's train was very heavy and Thomas had been working hard all day. He was very tired but he didn't want to let Edward down, so he **puffed** and **chuffed** and **huffed** along, as fast as he could.

When Thomas pulled into Knapford Station, The Fat Controller was waiting. "Why are you pulling this train?" he asked. "Where is Edward?"

"Er, he took on the wrong sort of coal ..." said Thomas.

"THE WRONG SORT OF COAL!"

boomed The Fat Controller. "Nonsense, Thomas! I'll speak to Edward about this later!"

He was so cross that he gave poor Thomas **another** job to do.

When Thomas didn't come back for him, Edward wheezed slowly home.

He stopped for a rest and Gordon told him what The Fat Controller had said to Thomas.

Edward felt very bad. He wanted to put things right, so he **hissed** and **wheezed** all the way to Knapford. His fire felt feeble. His wheels felt weak, but he didn't give up.

When he puffed into the station he spoke to The Fat Controller. "It's all my fault," he said. "I asked Thomas not to tell anyone I couldn't work. I was afraid of being no use and being sent for scrap."

"You should always tell me if you have a problem," said The Fat Controller. "You are a hard-working engine, Edward. A Really Useful Engine. You must go to the Fitter's Yard right away. They'll mend you and you'll be back at work in no time at all."

Thomas went with Edward, who was happy again now that he knew he'd soon be as good as new.

Thomas and Edward had both learned an important lesson that day.

"Even when it's hard ..." said Edward.

"It's always best to tell the truth!" said Thomas. **"Peeeep!"**

Percy and the funfair

The engines were excited. It was the day of The Fat Controller's funfair and all the children were coming to enjoy the rides.

There was lots to do! The Fat Controller went to Tidmouth to give the engines their jobs.

"Edward, you bring the merry-go-round," said The Fat Controller. "Henry, you can look after the roller-coaster. Gordon will bring the funfair people and Toby will collect the bumper cars. James and Emily will pull the big Ferris wheel."

Thomas wondered what his job would be. "Thomas, I want you to collect the fireworks and the Chinese Dragon!" said The Fat Controller.

"What's my job, Sir?" asked Percy.

"I want you to collect coal from the Coaling Plant, Percy," said The Fat Controller. "You must fill the hoppers at all the stations. A railway can't run without coal! This is a Very Important job."

Percy didn't think so! "Coal …" he sighed as he watched his friends steam away.

Percy felt left out as he chuffed to the Coaling Plant. Collecting coal was dull. "I wish I was pulling something exciting," he grumbled. "Not boring old coal trucks!"

Percy buffered up, then pulled out of the depot.

He stopped at the signal near the school playground.

Toby puffed past pulling the bumper cars. The children clapped and cheered when they saw him.

Then Edward chuffed by with the merry-go-round. The children cheered even louder.

Seeing his friends gave Percy an idea. "Toby and Edward need help!" he said. "Helping friends is more important than delivering coal!"

Naughty Percy didn't deliver the coal! He left his trucks and steamed after his friends.

He caught up with Toby and Edward at a red signal.

"Do you need some help?" Percy peeped.

"No thank you, Percy," said Toby.

"We can do it!" chuffed Edward.

"Oh," said Percy.

Further up the line Percy saw Emily and James with the Ferris wheel.

"I'm sure they need some help!" he peeped.

He caught up with Emily and James. But they said they didn't need any help.

Gordon was waiting at a junction with the funfair workers when Percy puffed up to him. But Gordon didn't need any help either.

Percy saw Henry on the bridge with the roller-coaster. But he didn't need any help.

Thomas was waiting at a signal when Percy puffed up. Thomas was carrying the fireworks and the big Chinese Dragon. But he didn't need Percy's help.

Percy felt sad and unwanted. Then there was trouble …

The engines needed more coal. But Percy hadn't delivered it!

"There's no coal at the stations!" James told him. "We've all run out!"

"Bust my boiler!" cried Percy. "If the engines don't get coal, there won't be a funfair, and it's all my fault!"

Percy knew what he had to do. He picked up his trucks and took coal to all the stations on Sodor. He went as fast as his wheels would carry him.

Soon all his friends' boilers were bubbling and their pistons were pounding again. The engines were **back on track!**

Percy did his last delivery and got to the funfair just in time to see the fireworks. Rockets soared, the band played, and the Chinese Dragon danced.

Everyone had a lovely time!

"The Fat Controller was right," peeped Percy happily. "Delivering the coal **was** a Very Important job."

· Percy and the Left Luggage ·

Percy really loves the summer time. He's as happy as can be when the sun shines!

One day, The Fat Controller talked to Percy about the jobs he needed him to do.

"I want you to collect the holiday mail, and deliver the lights that will light up the Town Hall," he said. "Then you can take the children to their summer party."

And that wasn't all!

"Please collect Dowager Hatt's luggage from Maithwaite Station and take it to the Airport," said The Fat Controller. "You must get it there on time."

"Yes, Sir!" peeped Percy, puffing off as fast as he could.

Soon, Percy stopped at the junction. The left track went to Maithwaite Station, where Dowager Hatt's luggage was waiting. The Postal Depot was straight ahead.

Percy thought about which way to go. But not for very long.

"Taking the luggage is an easy job," he said. **"I'll do that later."**

So Percy puffed straight ahead and collected the holiday mail.

He took mail to lots of stations. A wagon was uncoupled at each one, until all the deliveries were done.

When he came to the junction, Percy wondered what job to do next.

Straight ahead was Maithwaite Station and Dowager Hatt's luggage. The left track went to Brendam Docks, where the lights for the Town Hall were waiting for collection.

"Taking the luggage is an easy job," said Percy. **"I'll do that later."**

So Percy steamed off to the Docks to collect the lights. Then he took them to the Town Hall.

"Now I can take the children to the summer party!" peeped Percy. "That's the best job of all!"

Percy chuffed off as fast as he could.

He collected the children, then stopped to take on water.

While he was waiting at the water tower, The Fat Controller drove by in his car. He was taking Dowager Hatt to the Airport!

Oh, no! Percy had forgotten all about Dowager Hatt's luggage.

Her suitcases and bags were still waiting to be collected from Maithwaite Station!

"Bust my buffers!" he cried. "I must collect the luggage! But if I do that, who will take the children to the summer party? **Oh, I need some help!"**

Percy saw Edward in a siding. "Edward, will you take the children to the party for me, please?" asked Percy.

"Of course I will!" chuffed Edward, kindly.

As soon as Edward was coupled up to the children's coach, Percy rushed off to Maithwaite Station.

He buffered up to the luggage car, then he wheeshed away as fast as his wheels would carry him. He had to get to the Airport before The Fat Controller!

Percy raced along, puffing hard.
"Oh, why didn't I do this job first?" he cried.

Percy got to the Airport and the luggage was unloaded, just as The Fat Controller's car arrived.

"I made it on time!" peeped Percy, happily.

"Well done, Percy!" said The Fat Controller.

"You are a **Very Reliable Engine!**" said Dowager Hatt.

Phew! Percy smiled and blew his whistle, **"Peep!"** He would never leave things to the last minute again!

Keeping up with James

It was winter on the Island of Sodor and the hills and houses, bridges and branch lines, stations and signalboxes were all covered in a white snowy blanket.

Workmen were fitting the engines with snowploughs in the Fitter's Yard. "We have to keep the railway running so you must work in pairs," The Fat Controller told the engines.

"**Gordon** will work with **Emily**, **Toby** will work with **Henry**, **Percy** will work with **Thomas** – and **James** will work with **Edward**," said The Fat Controller. "Now remember, the tracks are very icy and you must all **take care**!"

The Fat Controller had something else to tell them. "When the lines are clear, I want one of you to take the Presents Train to the Winter Party at Knapford."

ALL the engines wanted to do that special job – especially James. But he didn't want to do it with Edward. "He's an old slowcoach," he huffed. "He'll just slow me down!"

Thomas felt sorry for Edward. "Don't worry," he told him. "There's more to being a Really Useful Engine than being fast."

Later, James and Edward were clearing the lines to Knapford. Edward chugged along slowly and steadily.

He wasn't fast enough for James, who huffed past him and peeped loudly. **"Hurry up!"**

James rushed past Gordon and Emily.

"Slow down!" called Gordon.

"Take care!" cried Emily.

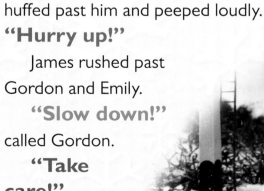

But James took no notice. He was thinking about the Presents Train, not the icy tracks, and his wheels began to slip and slide!

"Whooooooaah!" he cried as he went faster and faster. He liked going fast so he slid all the way to Knapford Station, where men were putting up the Christmas decorations.

Edward arrived much later. "Trust you to be late!" James huffed. "We're taking coal trucks to the mines and you are to be the back engine. I'll show you how to go fast!"

As soon as Edward buffered up to the trucks, James pulled out and raced off. **"Must-be-first! Must-be-first!"** he puffed.

When he got to the top of Gordon's Hill, his boiler **bubbled** and his pistons **pumped**. Then his wheels started to slip and slide on the icy tracks and he sped down the hill.

"Wheee!" cried James. "This is how you go fast!"

Poor Edward was pulled down the hill.

He put on his brakes as hard as he could but then **his** wheels started to slip and **both** of them slid all the way down the hill!

"You must slow down and **take care**," Edward told James.

"I **am** taking care," said James. "Taking care to go **fast** and finish my jobs **first**. Then I'm going to pull the **Presents Train**!"

James set off for the Docks, dreaming of the Presents Train. **"Finish-first! Finish-first!"** he puffed, going faster and faster.

When he came to a bend in the track, James put on his brakes to slow down but his wheels slipped and slid. **"Oh, my!"** he cried.

Edward braked so hard that his wheels **wobbled** and his axles **squeaked**. But it was too late, and James and two of the coal trucks came off the rails!

"Burst my buffers!" said James.

When The Fat Controller arrived on Salty he was **NOT** pleased with James and Edward. "You did not **take care** as I told you!" he boomed.

James felt bad. "The crash wasn't Edward's fault," he said. "He wanted to slow down but I wanted to go fast so I could pull the Presents Train."

"Well, you won't be pulling it now!" said The Fat Controller. "Edward, **YOU** can pull the Presents Train. I'll find a back engine for you."

"If I promise to go slowly and **take care**, can I be Edward's back engine?" asked James.

"Very well," said The Fat Controller.

Edward and James collected the Presents Train from the Docks.

"Slow down!" called Edward when they came to icy patches on the track. And this time **James slowed down**.

"Put on your brakes!" called Edward when they ran down Gordon's Hill. And this time **James put on his brakes**.

The children were waiting at Knapford Station and when Edward and James steamed in, everyone cheered.

"Thank you for letting me help, Edward," said James happily. "You are a **Really Useful Engine!**"

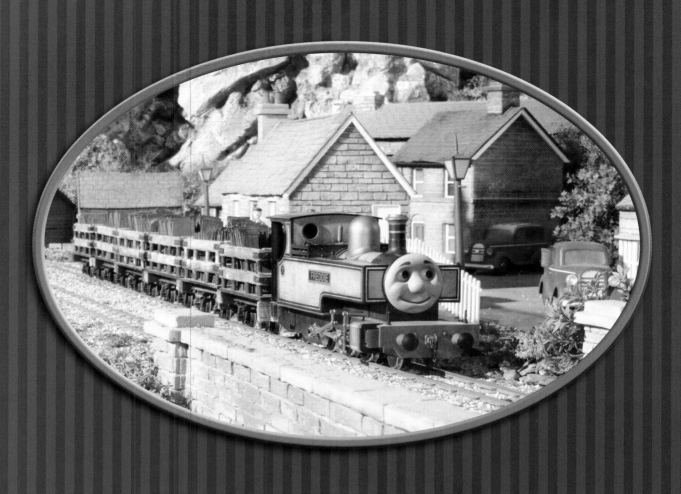